My Brother Oscar Thinks He Knows It All

By Linda Wagner Tyler

Pictures by Susan Davis

Puffin Books

PUFFIN BOOKS
Published by the Penguin Group
Viking Penguin, a division of Penguin Books USA Inc.,
375 Hudson Street, New York, New York 10014, U.S.A.
Penguin Books Ltd, 27 Wrights Lane, London W8 5TZ, England
Penguin Books Australia Ltd, Ringwood, Victoria, Australia
Penguin Books Canada Ltd, 10 Alcorn Avenue, Toronto, Ontario, Canada M4V 3B2
Penguin Books (N.Z.) Ltd, 182–190 Wairau Road, Auckland 10, New Zealand

Penguin Books Ltd, Registered Offices: Harmondsworth, Middlesex, England

First published in the United States of America by Viking Penguin Inc. 1989
Published in Picture Puffins, 1991
3   5   7   9   10   8   6   4   2
Text copyright © Linda Wagner Tyler, 1989
Illustrations copyright © Susan Davis, 1989
All rights reserved

Library of Congress Catalog Card Number: 90-53662
ISBN 0-14-050947-X

Printed in the United States of America
Set in Souvenir Light

For my brothers Paul and Tom with love and admiration. — L.W.T.

For my older sisters Patty and Mary Lib who actually did know it all. — S.D.

My brother Oscar is two years older than me.
He thinks I can't do anything right.

I'm still learning how to skateboard.

Oscar's an expert.

I lose all of my pieces when we play checkers.

Oscar saves all of his and so Oscar always wins.

I have training wheels on my bike.

Oscar can ride with no hands.

At the dinner table Oscar says, "Chew with your
mouth closed," which I always do.

He claims the best part of the tree house

and tells me it's too dangerous up there,

but I can bring him a soda.

When we make pictures for grandma he always

grabs the best stickers.

When Oscar's friend comes over

they make me go away.

But after his friend leaves

Oscar wants to play with me.

"Let's play school," he says.

"I'm the teacher and you have to stay after."

When *my* best friend comes over
Oscar has to show off.

"Who wants to see a great magic show?"
he says and he pulls out his tricks.

But every now and then I give Oscar a big surprise.

Like last week when we had a special sports
day at school.

Oscar and all of his friends were watching.

I finished first in the sack race.

Then in the running race I beat

all the boys and won that too.

Oscar and his friends all came running over
to see my blue ribbons.

"You were great!" they said.

That night Oscar told my dad, "She was the star of the day!

And *I* taught her all she knows."

Then he said, "You're pretty lucky to have me for a brother." But I know he is the lucky one to have a sister like me.